One Day I Closed My Eyes
and the World Disappeared

Elizabeth Bram

The Dial Press • New York

The Dial Press
1 Dag Hammarskjold Plaza
New York, New York 10017

Copyright © 1978 by Elizabeth Bram
All rights reserved · First Printing
Printed in the United States of America
Typography by Atha Tehon

Library of Congress Cataloging in Publication Data
Bram, Elizabeth.
One day I closed my eyes and the world disappeared.
Summary: A young girl closes her eyes and uses her
other senses to experience her surroundings.
(1. Senses and sensation—Fiction) I. Title.
PZ7.B73570n   (E)   77-86271
ISBN 0-8037-6611-4
ISBN 0-8037-6613-0 lib. bdg.

for mitzi

One day I closed my eyes
and the world disappeared.

I couldn't see trees

or streams

or stars.

But I could still feel things.
I could feel the sun

and wind

and wet grass

and mud.

I could smell flowers

and wood burning in the fireplace

and bread baking

and a pine tree

and my mother's perfume.

I could still hear things too.
I could hear a train go by.

I could hear my cat meow.

I could hear someone
walking down the stairs.

I could hear the leaves moving
against each other in the wind

and my brother
playing scales on the cello.

I could even hear myself breathing.

I could taste things too.
I could taste the sourness
of lemonade

and the sweetness of raisins.

I could even taste my own finger.

And when I opened my eyes again,
I could see trees

and streams

and stars.

The world had all come back.